THE BOOKSTORE BURGLAR

by **Barbara Maitland**

pictures by **Nadine Bernard Westcott**

SCHOLASTIC INC.

New York   Toronto   London   Auckland   Sydney
Mexico City   New Delhi   Hong Kong   Buenos Aires

For Catherine, Elizabeth,
Louis, and Hogan—B.M.

For Becky—N.B.W.

ISBN 0-439-29150-X

Text copyright © 2001 by Barbara Maitland.
Illustrations copyright © 2001 by Nadine Bernard Westcott.
All rights reserved.
Published by Scholastic Inc., 557 Broadway, New York, NY 10012,
by arrangement with Puffin Books, a member of Penguin Putnam Inc.
SCHOLASTIC and associated logos are trademarks and/or
registered trademarks of Scholastic Inc.

12 11 10 9 8 7 6 5 4 3 2 1   2 3 4 5 6 7/0

Printed in the U.S.A.   24

First Scholastic printing, October 2002

Chapter One

Mr. Brown owned a store.

It was not just any store.

It was a bookstore.

It was called the Black Cat Bookstore

Mr. Brown lived above the store

with his cat, Cobweb.

Cobweb was not just any cat.

Her best friends were mice.

Her favorite food was cheese.

Every morning Mr. Brown and Cobweb

ate cheese for breakfast.

Then they went downstairs

to open the store.

The Black Cat Bookstore

was not just any bookstore.

It sold only ghost books.

It even had a ghost!

Chapter Two

Cobweb liked to walk around the store.
She helped Mr. Brown keep an eye
on things.

One day, Cobweb saw something strange.

The spare key was not on its hook.

Then Cobweb saw a man with the key.

He was putting it in his pocket!

The man walked toward the door.

Only Cobweb knew what he had done.

"Stop him!" Cobweb said to the ghost.

"He's a burglar."

BANG! A book dropped on the man's head.

"Ouch!" he yelled.

Everyone came to see what had happened.

Cobweb stayed beside the empty hook.

She mewed.

But Mr. Brown didn't notice her.

SPARE KEY

"I'm very sorry," Mr. Brown told the man.

"My ghost made a mistake."

"What ghost?" said the man.

"This bookstore has a ghost," said a boy.

"It is a friendly ghost!"

"Ha! I don't believe in ghosts,"

said the man.

He left the store.

Chapter Three

Mr. Brown was busy all day.

He did not notice the empty hook.

At the end of the day, he closed the blinds.

Then he locked the door.

Cobweb mewed.

She jumped up by the hook.

She patted it.

"I'm too tired to play," said Mr. Brown.

"I'm going upstairs."

Cobweb stayed downstairs.

She thought the burglar

might come back.

It grew darker and darker.

Then she heard a key in the lock.

"That must be the burglar!" said Cobweb.

"Are you ready, ghost?"

Chapter Four

The burglar tiptoed across the store.

He had a flashlight.

BANG! A book fell off the shelf beside him.

"I don't believe in ghosts!" said the burglar.

Cobweb shook the blinds with her paws.

Rattle, rattle!

The burglar dropped his flashlight.

"Nice ghostie!" he said.

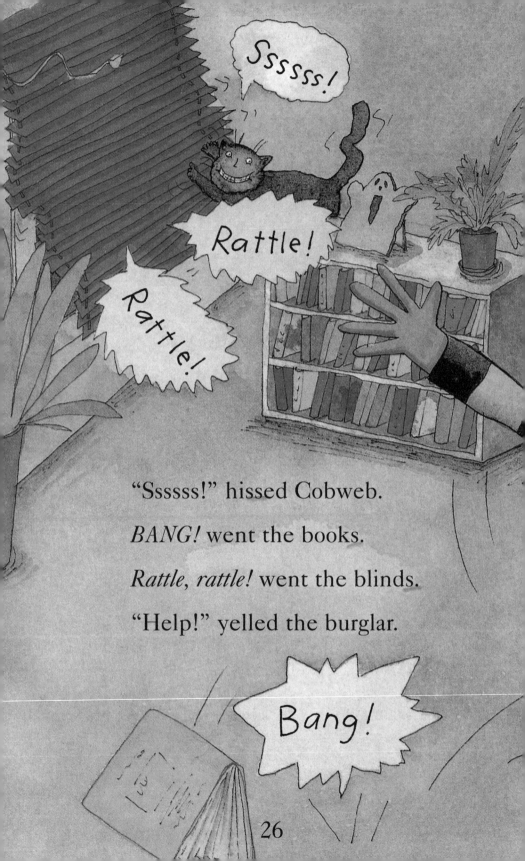

"Sssss!" hissed Cobweb.

BANG! went the books.

Rattle, rattle! went the blinds.

"Help!" yelled the burglar.

Chapter Five

Mr. Brown came downstairs.

"What's all this noise?" he asked.

He turned on the light

and saw the burglar.

"Your ghost is *not* friendly!"

yelled the burglar.

He ran out of the store.

Mr. Brown saw the spare key

in the door.

He saw the empty hook.

"So that's how the burglar

got in," he said.

"You tried to warn me.

Thank you, Cobweb."

"Thank you, too, ghost!" he told the mice.

"It's late.

You must be hungry.

Everyone follow me."

They went upstairs to the kitchen.

Mr. Brown made a treat.

It was not just any treat.

It was a cheese treat.

"I hope you like it," he said.

They did.